A Day at the Café

Butterbean's Café

By Kristen L. Depken • Illustrated by Francesco Legramandi and Gabriella Matta

Random House 🏠 New York

rhcbooks.com

ISBN 978-0-593-12189-4

MANUFACTURED IN CHINA

10 9 8 7 6 5 4 3 2 1

One morning at Butterbean's Café, Butterbean and her friends were getting ready for a party. The Bean Team was going to need lots of energy on this busy day, so Butterbean and Cricket made a special breakfast for them: fluttercakes!

After breakfast, the friends made the café look extra pretty for the party. "I'm just adding some finishing touches," Dazzle told Butterbean as she put a bunch of *fairy* fresh flowers on each table. They smelled amazing!

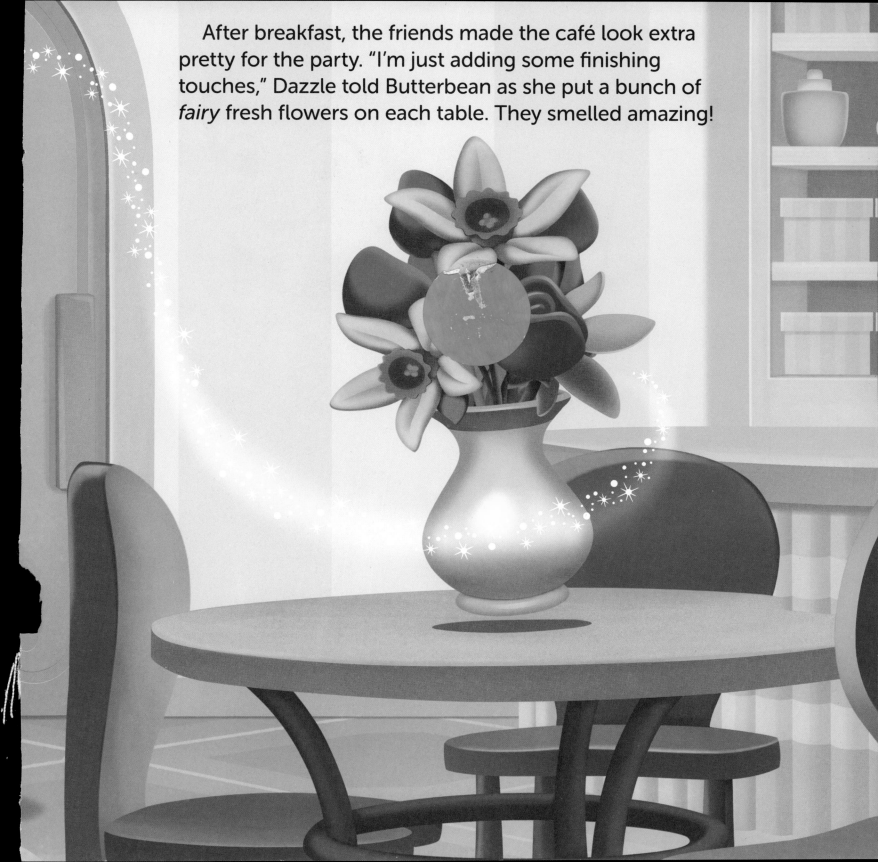

Butterbean had a great food plan for the party: strawberry honey cake, smoothies, pizza, and lemonade.
When Jasper arrived from the farm with a delivery of fresh fruit and vegetables, the team got to work!

Poppy used her magical spoon to measure the honey for the cake. She mixed the honey with butter, eggs, and flour before putting it all in the oven to bake.

Once the cake had cooled, Cricket piped on swirls of vanilla buttercream before topping it with ripe strawberries.

Meanwhile, Dazzle made fruit smoothies.
She blended bananas, mangoes, and pineapples
for a tasty tropical twist!

Butterbean, Cricket, and Poppy got to work on the pizza. First, they kneaded the dough. Then they made their own tomato sauce and spread it over the dough before sprinkling on some cheese and bell peppers.

It didn't take long before they had a delicious pizza that was ready to eat. It was time to take the food to the party!

Finally, Butterbean and her friends made *fairy* fresh lemonade. While they were busy in the kitchen, Mrs. Marmalady snuck into the café. She tried to ruin the party by pouring barbecue sauce onto the cake! Luckily, Cricket stopped her just in time.

It was party time! The guests loved the cake, smoothies, pizza, and fresh-squeezed lemonade. Everything had been prepared to perfection.

The Bean Team had done it again! Butterbean
thanked her friends for another great day at the café.